Nov. 11/92

THE

Richard

BOOKS BY RICHARD TRUHLAR

Figures in Paper Time
(The Mercury Press, 1989)

Utensile Paradise
(Aya Press, 1987)

Parisian Novels
(The Front Press, 1986)

Moon Dice
(Underwhich Editions, 1982)

A Porcelain Cup Placed There
(Coach House Press, 1979)

THE PITCH

Richard Truhlar

The Mercury Press

"Stet," first published in *Rampike*, 10th Anniversary Issue, Part 1,
Vol. 7, No. 1, Toronto, 1990
"The Pitch," first published in the *Capilano Review*,
No. 50, N. Vancouver, 1989
"Fact Simile," first published in *paragraph*,
Vol. 13, No. 2, Stratford, Ontario, 1991

The author is grateful for the financial assistance of the Ontario Arts Council and the City of Toronto through the Toronto Arts Council.

The Mercury Press acknowledges the financial assistance of the Canada Council and the Ontario Arts Council as well as that of the Ontario Ministry of Culture and Communications through the Ontario Publishing Centre.

Cover Photo: Paul Till
Cover Design: Gordon Robertson
Author Photo: André Pierre Leduc
Typeset in Antiqua and Avant Garde by TASK
Printed and bound in Canada

Canadian Cataloguing in Publication

Truhlar, Richard, 1950-
The pitch

ISBN 0-920544-86-X

I. Title.

PS8589.R83P58 1992 C813'.54 C92-094536-8
PR9199.3.T782P58 1992

The Mercury Press
137 Birmingham Street
Stratford, Ontario
Canada N5A 2T1

for John Riddell

"When I reflect on it now, I marvel that I nevertheless always managed wholly to return from the world of these fevers and to adjust myself to that thorough community of life, where each wanted support in feeling that he was among people he knew, and where one so carefully got on together in the comprehensible."

Rainer Maria Rilke
The Notebooks of Malte Laurids Brigge

"Wonder had gone away, he had forgotten that all life is only a set of pictures in the brain, among which there is no difference betwixt those born of real things and those born of inward dreamings..."

H.P. Lovecraft
The Silver Key

Contents

The Better Way

His left hand grips the chrome-plated post of a subway car which is speeding through a dark tunnel carved beneath the city streets, the image of a seven-year-old boy dropping on to steel tracks, that sudden silence in the breath of onlookers, the cold sensation of nothing before him, nothing happened really, nothing at all.

Just going to work, that's all, going along like everyone else, gripping the chrome-plated post with a sweaty hand because it's summer and one's hand tends to get sweaty in the summer if one's hand is holding on to something.

Gnawing at the cuticles around the nails of his right fingers, has he missed the stop? Staring at the advertisement posted above the sliding doors, THE BETTER WAY, he loses his balance for a moment as the subway car jerks, staring at the faces staring into space, reading paperbacks and newspapers, trying to escape each other's eyes.

Impatient, perhaps he should sit down?

Somebody pushes him and he thinks, no, he won't descend to their level, won't push somebody back, rather show courtesy, show the way he was brought up, the old values, whatever happened to the old values?

Sliding doors open and close and why is he always shoulder to shoulder with them? all sweating because it's summer and some of the older cars don't have air-conditioning but only upper windows which slide down to allow stale tunnel air to stream in, and there's always one more stop to go, or two or three, and it feels like waiting because he's become conscious of doing nothing, and he wants to act, but feels his facial muscles frozen in an expressionless expression and there's no reason to act anyway.

Once he was smiling and didn't know it, when he noticed them staring at him, then turning their eyes away quickly, and he tried to be inconspicuous as he glanced at his fly... no... then perhaps I'm bleeding, he thought, had he unconsciously picked at some boil on his face and now there's a red blossom turning into a thin trickle? or perhaps... looking at his hands... the newspaper he'd been reading, fresh ink and when he sneezed that time— left a black mark on the tip of his nose.

Suddenly he remembers the look on that face, face of a seven-year-old in front of him on the platform, in front of him, a small hand catching at air, a mouth opening with no sound, and trying to remember what that face said, was it Mommy or Daddy, don't leave me or help me? and falling away from him and knowing the train can't stop in time, everyone's jostling for position, to be up front when the doors open, to get a seat because one's legs get sore standing, but you're going to be standing for awhile aren't you? he thinks, because they have to clean up before the train moves on.

But didn't anyone see it? he wonders, or perhaps it's like that time he was seated on a bus and suddenly went cold with fear because he couldn't remember if he had arisen from his seat for a moment, crossed the aisle and molested that pretty girl seated across from him, and everyone else in the bus knew he'd done it except... he couldn't remember.

But now the train is moving, and he's on his way, should be at work soon, should begin thinking about work now, all of them thinking about work now, not about the seven-year-old, probably didn't really happen, just the strength of his imagination, but now can't rid of himself of a feeling of helplessness, imagining small hands catching at air, to grip on to something, hold on to someone, why can't he hold on to someone? always separated by space, alone in his body, apart from others, the need continually arising in him to squash others to his chest, fuse his body into another's, commingle minds and souls, feel the presence of another within his flesh, within his thoughts, never to be alone again, never always arms flailing or hanging loosely, empty... he notices, the subway car is empty but for him, the subway car speeding, the subway car not stopping, stations left behind, coming up and left behind, and his sweaty hand feels cold now gripping the chrome, and so much time has passed he feels so much time has passed and he should be getting off soon but in a flash he thinks I'm going to hell, he's going to hell in a subway car and it doesn't matter if he's done nothing wrong, anyone can go to hell in a subway car, seven-year-olds go to hell under subway cars, and parents go to hell remembering seven-year-olds going to hell under subway cars, and we were always told: it's the third rail, don't touch the third rail, or you fry.

And when the car doors finally slide open, he forgets about going to hell. He's going up now, going up escalators now, going to catch a streetcar, another car on tracks, sometimes stopped in its tracks with small bones tangled on steel wheels, going up to catch a streetcar which he boards, sits down in, slides up the window, feels the air stream in, rests his arm on the windowsill, the sill with the small brass plaque which reads KEEP ARM IN and he is driven to stick his head far out the window just as another oncoming streetcar on the opposite track speeds by or to throw his briefcase out the window so he'll have to get off and catch a later car and so waste time.

But he doesn't. Instead he thinks of pronouns, we're all just pronouns, seven-year-olds are pronouns with adjectives attached, adjectives like *small* or *frail*, and the air streaming in the window feels cold on his sweaty skin, and this is an adjective too, he thinks, the cold sensation of nothing before him, nothing before him but for perhaps another *small* body to be pushed, the future of another *frail* body to be pushed into the tide of oncoming death, his own death frozen in the verb *push*, in the sudden silence of breathless onlookers as his hand reached out for the boy and nothing happened, nothing at all.

Stet

I went to cross out father's name from my address book since he had died and such an address is no longer useful, but I let it stand.

I cross out many things, cross out words, cross out commas and parentheses, cross out entire lives, entire paragraphs, cross out lies and cross out truths, begin and end histories, make sure facts are concise, properly represented, every punctuation marking the correctly measured pause.

It was just that one day, a few days after his death, I scanned the obituaries and found a listing, so many names passing into history, a continuum of text dying into tomorrow.

How many days does it take for a name to die, to pass into back-issues, microfilm or data-banks in library holdings? If I went to the library, I could find father's name, just as I could find my own under *Births*.

It was that one day though, when I went to cross out father's name and simultaneously noticed the plethora of obituaries, that I saw another name, a simple name, not at all significant but recognizable.

Yes, I recognized that name because I had crossed it out. It hadn't seemed important to the text I was assembling. A bystander perhaps or peripheral figure in the scenario, in the item I had to construct from sketchy notes, a figure not important as far as I could see, so deleted.

And suddenly to appear again the next day, that name, with the time of the service, the names of those he had left behind, a sentimental tribute, final flourish and good-bye.

History had been made.

I make history. Every day I make it, form it into a readable substance, allow it a little rein then pull it in before it becomes too restless. Readers can't stand restlessness, need to have just the facts, right there in front of them first thing in the morning as they're having their coffee and shedding the aura of sleep.

They all need to know, just like I need to know, and I know best when I have made history. I feel secure knowing I have control, limited control albeit, but control nevertheless over how history will appear the next day.

Of course, one cannot rely on typesetters. They can change history, distort it for the briefest moment— a word misspelled and *sects* becomes *sex*: morality is thrown into a questionable position upon the page, readers being refracted from the perfection of history they are intent upon absorbing.

But a name crossed out before making history is different. It's considered, weighed, authenticated— no improvisation or ambiguity is present— it's out.

In or out— this is the leverage of the professional history maker. Applied each day with the appropriate pressure and I'm assured of an avid readership.

But on that one day, I recognized that name. It had not died, had simply been crossed out, a bystander. Can't have too many bystanders in history. It obscures the facts, so I crossed the name out.

Yet it was there the next day, but not where I had not put it. Another page and another page had to be turned before it was found out. It was hiding there, even though it was supposed to be living, hiding there in *Obituaries*.

And I was forced to think of the orbit of a name, how it appears on birth certificates, circulates amongst friends, is hired, appears on bank statements, and finally declares itself dead.

I deal in names every day, but when they're declared dead I can think only of decay—you were once there, weren't you? but not today, today you're declared in moving tribute, festschrift for a passing and arbitrary collection of the alphabet making a particular sound as it passes from mouth into print while you raise your head from your reading since someone has articulated that which you have come to call yourself.

So when I crossed out your name, I had no idea you would appear the next day, printed before my eyes, the only eyes to recognize that you shouldn't have appeared there.

But there you were.

Was there something I didn't know about you? How could you evade my control and escape on to another page? Did I deserve such humiliation at the hands of a name?

The story was a simple one, didn't make the front page and so doesn't bear repeating, except that you had nothing to do with it. You were peripheral and insignificant to the story and so you were crossed out.

But there you were the next day, as if it had happened to you, as if you had been seated at that table where the bomb was detonated or had crossed that intersection where the milk truck ran you down or in that last searing moment of denial had thrown yourself on to those tracks feeling the mounting pressure of air forced from the subway tunnel.

I wasn't there, have only notes of what you were reported to have said, an eye-witness account, but who needs to quote you when the facts were obvious, and you said "It was like this...", but that was apparent, had been reported over and over by a number of onlookers, so your quote was redundant and so were you, so you were deleted. It wasn't necessary to go on at length. Repetition can be of value in an item, but too much of it can dismay a reader.

Standing before your coffin, I wouldn't have been able to look at you, or perhaps for just a moment, seeing the cosmetic glow of an after-history.

Everyone else is crying, but I refer to my notes. Perhaps you weren't even there since your name escapes me now. I look down into your coffin and remember writing the story. Your name wasn't in it. If your name had been in it, would I have been a pall-bearer? When they took you from the hearse into the church, you were of normal weight as you lay in your coffin. When I returned you to the hearse after the service, I could hardly manage to help carry you, my hands weak, grip failing, letting you slide, coffin tumbling to the ground, lid falling open, cosmetic glow rolling out on to the pavement, expecting you to get up, brush the dirt from your carefully pressed suit as if you were alive but merely groggy from too much sleep.

I've re-read your name. You were the bystander, someone not important, insignificant, someone to cross out— in or out— this is the leverage of the professional history maker. How many days does it take a name to die?

The Pitch

It began on a business trip, not a normal disorientation, sense of isolation, but face after face chatting, eating, securing the worth of the voyage from the fragile ego fluttering against glass to escape those frozen moments of recognition. Memory comes back, a stranger met on the plane, "I'm sorry, I've forgotten your name...", and you find yourself gazing into the mirror once too often, but you continue shaving, brush your teeth, all the while feeling this body below you, somehow not connected to the feet firmly planted on bathroom tiles.

Leafing through the *Yellow Pages* in search of a bathhouse with yellow women who will soap your skin, lay hands upon, give some sense of the solidity of body you wish you could feel... only to end up gazing at the names of bookstores, having already bought more than you can read, the silence of the hotel room you sit voiceless within and ambient hum of unseen technology behind the walls or in the ceiling, not enough to distract you, however, from the silence you feel within yourself.

It's too early to eat, you think, as you pull on your overcoat, your body moving without thought, can't stay here, the door locking itself behind you, your hand automatically checking to feel for the key in your vest pocket, wouldn't want to be shut out, then out you go, incessant need for motion, not helping it, following it... perhaps if I walk far enough, exhaust myself, I'll be able to relax, fall back into the room, cushy pillow to support my back, take up another novel, pore over each page forgetting where I am, why I'm here.

Each time you come to this place, at least once you visit that special spot, that urban beach which looks out upon the sea, and you smoke and think and tell yourself that you must appreciate the vista: those mountains! that ocean! smell that!... for a moment you remember some other time when you were a boy and somehow you can't remember where it was, how you were a boy, but the smell and what was it? some mixture now forgotten but holding you as you move to the water's edge, pick out a few seashells washed up before you arrived, colourful enough you hope, take them back for the boy, hope he likes them, tell him where they're from, this bay, describe something he's never seen... and each time you come to this place, you come alone, each time wishing there was another to share this place... you walk away. This place cannot be had. If you... you always look back, the vista, wanting to take it with you, looking back, walking but stopping more frequently, knowing the next vista obliterates the latter into memory, memory never a postcard you can send back to yourself... so you always return, every time you come to this city, sit on that beach, look out, get up, walk on, look back, stopping more frequently, wishing you could print yourself, say "See!" and perhaps they would all understand, would all come along the next time, the room opening up, becoming a house, a loving hand soaping your back, face passing by an open door... "Hi!", but not forgotten.

You get up, look up, yes, there are the mountains, the rippled glass of water before you, gazing into a mirror once too often you have found yourself upon this beach remembering the silent room from which you issued, perhaps it's time to eat?

On the sidewalk you pause before a restaurant menu posted outside, try to be inconspicuous, nonchalant, not wanting to commit yourself, diners inside staring at you. Am I really hungry? do I go in? look down the street, perhaps walk a little farther, find somewhere else, just the place you want: warm, friendly, a waitress who smiles, relaxes your cold coat on to the empty seat across from you, poring over the menu, forced decisions from hunger and looking out at the water, remembering how it was to sit and watch from your bench the seagull peck at the sand, fly off with a dinosaur scream remembering some forgotten appointment.

You look at your wristwatch, the digital face of death somehow absent from your gaze, seeing yourself after the third martini not wanting to move, watching the sun separate itself from your consciousness, move into the idea of its breaking through the clouds.

Appointments are made, and the room calls you back, "Sorry not 10:30," sitting but not at a beach, brought back some shells, one unopened, dead but unopened and what's inside? probably rotting, stashed it in your luggage, probably will open on the way home, the smell of more than the sea reminding you how you carried it around for hours, the other open shells in your pocket, this one in my hand, will the warmth of my hand make a difference? open the unopened, warm air escaping, liquid running out on to my palm, smell it, smell the beach, me sitting there wanting to stay, wanting to move... carried it for hours, back to the room, wrapped it and the other shells in a plastic shower cap, tied it tightly, no gas escapes, no stench, no reminder, just get it back and perhaps the boy asking why it hadn't opened and you saying you don't know but it's dead and let's hope it doesn't open because of the stink, the stink you hoped for in that room, the roll of the surf surging up, crashing against your bed where you're alone with your cock in your hand wishing for wetness, looking at the digital face of your wristwatch and wondering when they'll phone, if they will, and wishing every chambermaid had yellow skin, would soap your back, giggle when in jest you splashed water from the bath like a child, your own child, face of your own child meeting you in the mirror, the brief flash of a smile, your feet firmly planted on bathroom tiles and "hi dad!", the roll of the surf against your mind, I can relax.

Skin Shoe, Long Pig

Wearing a white wide-rimmed straw hat, she sits now in the garden. Totally forgotten are the managers, the operators, the regulators. Confronted by administrative and professional problems, she had plunged into the ungrateful world of causes and allegiances.

She puts things away, takes them out, puts them away again. "I never mind doing the cooking." She sits in the garden and puts things away. "Everything is eaten with potatoes," she remembers, the delicacy of fresh sliced fruit, mint and meringue. "That word spoken is the wrong way to eat."

Palm leaves and sand, steaming logs of meat rolled out on to thick blankets, coarse-haired, everything used in the feast.

Arising from her lawn-chair, she moves indoors, the house carefully articulated by furniture, known objects. Her body works on itself from within, the vaporous noise of the inner body caused by the pleasure of anticipation while she imagines virile dark meats, asparagus, celery, truffles, vanilla. "A cup of vinegar each day" and she's slimmer now.

Relief agency, institution in the utopian mode, feeds the hungry, the starving. Whenever desire has an object, put the body back from where it has been taken. She was the one to prepare and serve but not eat. "The woman does not eat, rather she rustles in the toss of lettuce, the sauté of lean meat, the dicing of crisp vegetables," her doctor advising her against soup and beer.

There were never any maggots, everything eaten quickly, nothing wasted. WE ARE THE FOOD OF THE FUTURE, she had read and applied for the job the next day. Three months later, she was not distracted but concentrated, alert but silent where nicotine and caffeine eyes stared a yellow look of fish, oyster, quinine water. Her home had been different, ordered, not this haphazard mixture of mud and bones baked into walls, merely shelters from the sun.

Shout of mouth, shout of bowel, "Eat with your hands," that deep central zone of the desert, she apart from her manner of good breeding, the digestion of soft permeable meal.

Once inside, she puts things away, takes them out again, she is the one who prepares and serves but does not eat. Her kitchen is immaculate, noiseless, immovable. Wandering through the furniture, she momentarily glances at her writing desk. The cookbook she wishes to complete has narcotic power, the sizzle of pages turned each time a new dish is distinguished, a great noise within her waiting to rustle forth, evaporate into an erotic tremble.

Watching the dope-smokers gather into groups around their fires, the wisps of not speaking well and wine on their breaths, taking coffee, she remembers the dark sauces caught in the throat, can't talk through the eating, each lick lap bite: part of a vocabulary of the body consumed, of a civilization for which she was not responsible, she putting things away, the body missing from every bouquet, meat slipping effortlessly from the bone beside emerald green plastic bags stencilled in red ink FOOD.

A collapsing soufflé of bones and sauce cooked quickly over open fire in a recipe for small talk, a whiff of language passed out as cutlery; and she was watching, not distracted but concentrated, alert but silent.

"Aren't the flowers lovely this afternoon?", she pointing out to her friend how lucky they were to be living where they lived, "There were never any maggots," living amidst the eating industry of the future. "Skin shoe, skull cap, necessary you know for crossing the desert," she snipping some fresh chives for the salad.

"A sort of alcohol of meat," she later announces, moving nearer to her writing-desk, the overwhelming noise of smells and tastes imagined in dry ink, the dinner guests quickly exchanging glances, brows furrowing, "and now for a true change of taste...", the sizzle of pages turned, nicotine and caffeine eyes apart from her manner of good breeding, never having written it down, "I present...", because it would've become a great gaping silence through which the world would fall, "long pig!"

She is sitting in the garden wearing a white wide-rimmed straw hat. "I never mind doing the cooking," and in that deep central zone of the desert, she is the one who prepares and serves but does not eat.

Assimulator

You are a surgeon, right wrist immobilized, strapped down for intravenous feeding, oxygen tube to your mouth.

It had started just below the breast-bone. You put out a half-smoked cigarette, the pain dull, momentarily reflecting on the hidden progress of a disease. Another attack, of course, is possible. The present mass of trajectories across cardiograph paper— a suspended death sentence.

When you finally lift your head, you discover five amplifiers taped to your chest. What on the x-ray had looked like a dark stain the size of a man's fist...?

Quite a ritual, you think, the incision perceived with exceptional clarity, your mind detached as if your head were severed, cannot sense a movement throughout your torso. You are *not* going to drift off again! falling into a zombie sleep, your legs walking you to destinations, meetings you have no interest in. In the depths of your body, you are to lie down immediately.

The tumour was pronounced malignant and had corroded a part of yourself beyond repair, a part of yourself replaced with another, coiled now within you, waiting to unfold into movement, purpose, be born apart from its temporary hibernation.

Transplanted from the hospital to home, you watch the landscape through the car's rear-view mirror, an incision into time, the bladder-bag of your mind aching to piss out its terror of words you resist acknowledging.

Who was the other? the other's part planted in you to continue yesterday and tomorrow, another's time, another's place... did it laugh, did it cry, had it been caressed with good-night kisses?

Blood vessels expand, you breathe more easily, yet feel as though it belongs to someone else. Before the bathroom mirror, delicately you run a finger along the blood-red stripe from breast-bone to abdomen sensing the incision into the various roles which constitute you, the whole body caving in, crumbling away beneath your hands trying frantically to persuade pieces of yourself from falling on to the bathroom tiles by hugging your chest, gripping your bowels.

The awareness begins while holding a slice of bread, buttered, cigarette paper clinging to the sole of one shoe, left eye twitching from exhausted ganglia. That's it, yes that's *it*! the shape in you, a thing unnamed, instant of self-contradiction while suicide bounces a ball in your head.

Enclosed, not just beneath the skin, soft and entangled, a body works from within, your lips glistening, teeth biting into a partridge wing, crystallized, candied, a chemistry fizzing into a perception of yourself as food, an internal need to drink, to classify, transgress. You are other than you appear.

A surgeon once, you remember, at the hospital... remembering the pedestrian utterance of colleagues, your practice resonating in the word *cutting*, scalpel always sharp, transforming aberrance into survival.

History begins with footsteps, the day you leave the hospital, separation of career and victim, the act of walking to the car overlooked. You feel it unnecessary to consider the contents of the diagnosis: I was ill, now I'm well.

At home, on the phonograph, Elgar's *Enigma Variations*, code of your ancestors, upbringing, the tea and gathered by the radio, speaking comfortably, father working on the ledger trying to balance expense against excess, ephemeral ticking of the metronome towards dissolution, yet *Enigma* confronting the continual caving in of flesh as it drops from the bone, erupts in the brain, is sent squirming across the operating-room floor, ankle-deep in blood and enigma echoing in the mind as the scalpel cuts, the sound of skin hissing open to reveal variations played out between organs, tissue, membrane...

At home, you are tending the azaleas, special hybrid, grafting other colours/shapes on to the familiar, when suddenly you fall into your late friend at the moment when a part of him failed to continue, exhausted, complicated, confused, his mind out of reach of instant self-contradiction, the parts worn down by over-usage, self-martyred entropic flesh dependent upon a continuous but corrupting metabolism.

...but it was *just* a transplant, you think, one foot before the other, the other part of you moving, stretching out, slowly, hungrily, stretching out from another like yourself, another necessity of continuance.

Once your fear passes: it was merely a transplant, a procedure you yourself are master of. You told no-one, reputation and social image of the utmost importance, self-complications a trivial matter. Others need not know, your mind encompassing other selves, the legs which take, the arms that reach, a head which pivots upon a long thick neck, while steaming inner air and liquids erode.

You are not allowed to defecate, to urinate— each morning awaking to find a thick green residue covering the entire surface of your skin, pores having become orifices of elimination, flesh turned inside out, your bowels a living space kept clean by its tenant, but *you* are not the landlord.

It has no eyes, you think, can not see me, yet senses its position within the whole, relates to its surroundings, has so far not compromised you. Its failure to adapt would place you in peril.

The shape remains the same— perhaps not the size, the age, its unseen colour— but the shape is organized, knows its past.

Many times you have cut into others. Prone and prepped for the blade, deciding on only local anaesthetic, wanting to watch that part of you removed, part of the other inserted, attached, like the greedy mouth of a parasite, you thought.

"Look here...", you say to her, "see that lump, what do you think it is?", she gently passing her fingers over it, "...it's not me," she looking at you quizzically, uncomprehending, "They said it was a tumour...", the sound of skin hissing open, "but now it's other," retrieving her hand as if it may be suddenly bitten.

Earfull

Sitting idly, absentmindedly picking his nose with his right index finger, his other hand lifting the glass of gin and tonic to his lips, all the while staring out at the shimmering sheet of hot air rising from the city asphalt. He thinks: a holiday, that's what I need. Get away from it all, from the stench, the noise, the combustible faceless people who jostle him wherever he's trying to make an entrance or exit; a holiday in a small town, where they'd invited him to come for a visit, spend a few days, ideal location, relax, do what I want when I want with no responsibilities; just a lazy little provincial town where one can stretch, walk, think or forget, the choice is mine.

Come on up, they'd said, so he did and it was just as they'd told him— ideal location, relaxed, do what I want, they do what they want; sometimes walking together, sometimes alone, the streets never crowded and faces friendly; taking coffee day or night at a nearby bistro, talking of art together or thinking alone.

One night he was left alone at the house, they having gone off for coffee, and he restless, not wanting to be in the house alone but not wanting to go off for coffee either, deciding to go out into the backyard, small backyard, surrounded by a fence, with a garden, and a plot of earth at the very back covered with small stones and dried leaves.

And a picnic table also near the back— ideal, he thinks, just as they said— ideal location, sitting on the picnic table, looking up at the dark sky full of stars, and alone, feeling distinctly alone, the cool air and it's very dark, very dark he thinks, can see shapes around me but not any detail, and silent, it's very silent, or nearly silent, his ears listening intently for sound around him, listening to hear if they had returned yet; but no, they would go for coffee for hours, and he would sit here a long time and let his senses stretch out, stretch out and try to make sense out of dark shapes, smell the damp earth from the garden, or listen intently for sound around him; but the word *silent* kept coming to him, and the dark shapes around him eluded any detailed scrutiny.

Everything rests at night, he thinks, then remembers *National Geographic* documentaries about creatures who are only active at night, so not everything rests at night, not everything he thinks as he listens intently for sound around him and begins to hear something he hadn't heard before, a faint racket coming from the direction of the plot of earth covered with small stones and dried leaves, just about six feet away from where he's sitting on the picnic table.

It's as if something is moving, but it's not just one thing because it's a racket of many minute sounds, a racket as if small stones were clicking up against one another or dried leaves were being pushed aside; and he stares at the spot, the spot from where the sound issues, and thinks that something must be growing, coming up from under ground; it's springtime, so that's the answer, just a bunch of plants growing up and pushing the surface debris aside.

But it must be growing very quickly because every now and then the faint racket grows louder and is no longer faint but distinct, made up of distinct sounds, aggressive, not slow growth but swift sharp motions making swift sharp sounds, and it's not clicking or rustling any more, but snapping, snapping like the teeth of some carnivore, and he's thinking this as he comes closer to the spot, two feet from the plot of earth where he's craned his neck out and is staring intently, concentrating, trying to see any motion along the small stones or dried leaves.

But nothing is moving, or at least not yet, but how can something make those sounds without moving? and he can't see anything moving, but he's not going to lower his head too close to the ground because it could erupt and grab his face, stick onto his face like a parasite and begin sucking at his eyes. Even now his feet are vulnerable, right at the edge of the plot of ground, and what if it moved towards him, if a long tubular lump of earth thrust itself on to his feet?

What would make such a racket? and suddenly it moved, the ground moved, or at least he thought it did, just for a moment, but not the plot of ground covered with small stones and dry leaves, but rather a piece of lawn three feet to the left of him seemed to swell up like an ocean wave throwing itself forward and then sink back again into a flat piece of lawn.

And he wanted to go back into the house, it was getting too noisy out here, too much jostling his nerves— that's it, he thinks, it's just my nerves, left-over residue in my nerves from the noise and jostle of the city, the city where he lives, where everything is always moving and making noise so that you wouldn't hear a faint racket in your backyard at night, you wouldn't know that something was growing beneath your feet or moving slowly towards you, colonizing and claiming the space around it, and you wouldn't see it because it's so small in such a big city and only comes out at night, and you can't hear it because your ears are already too full.

The Desert of the Real Itself

...as *in medias res* thinking parenthetically, and, you know, saying something significant about it all, you adjust your tie while she says something, your gaze adjusting itself to see beyond the window pane, the pain in your gaze going astray among memories of a winter's night, an open window, a small cat curling upon a wooden fence...

...she coming through an open door, you remembered an open window, a possibility of escape or entry, and how she smoked her cigarette, the open mouth white, simply white...

...snow on the sill and paw tracks, perhaps a canary sang that night, but no, that's imagined, it was just drunken liquid vowels dripping from your lips, how the party roared when they found out your words, believed whispered, but apparent and your part in their embarrassment, the clinking of silverware falling silent, how they all fell silent...

...the look in your eyes never seen by yourself, alone by yourself always saying to yourself, she says to you only the echoes in your head...

...no, it was that other night, a night of other speaking, saying how it reminded him so much of another speaking, and speaking similarities come to life, walk about the room, given attributes, characterized, as she looks this way/ he looked that way, can't you *see* how I feel, the feeling always escaping you into words, a mouth in motion covered up, and you helped her on with her coat, she saying thank you...

...thank you so much, and much grows denser and thinking is foiled, ready to roast in their eyes, every time you speak ignoring thinking, thinking you're hearing thinking as you speak, not needing to make connections, not make anything out of it...

...and suddenly interrupted as you're talking with one by another, turning your face slowly (a camera action you have rehearsed) so that the glue dripping from your gaze has time enough to adhere to another face, smiling, the face is always smiling, no pain in the pane of those eyes, just a miniature you in reflection, smiling back...

...in reflection a simile always occurs, a simile similar to other similes, but you keep talking anyway, any way the words will take you, and you don't care what they think of you since you're a thought already, and when away a memory sometimes...

...the telephone rings, and it's him/her— does it matter? this incision, this thought of you? I'm thinking of you right now, I've been thinking of you off and on, I've thought of you a lot lately, have you thought much about me? much collides with memory, their similitude only in alliteration, no consonance in their creation, to tell you the truth I haven't thought of you lately, I've been thinking of you often, I've just been thinking of you...

...you remember that time, not so long ago, when you remembered that time, and we both spoke of it, it was over coffee, pass the salt please, remember that time, the telephone rings, is it him/her? pass the salt please, hello thought, how are you? remembering to say fine while not particularly feeling...

...thinking all the while that he/she is there, right there where they're saying they are, on the other end of the phone, and thinking them seated or standing, smoking or smiling, and they needing to think of your speaking since you're absent, since there is no pane of your eyes within which to read your thoughts...

...you read my thoughts, how did you know what I was thinking? we must think alike, like thoughts, existing like thoughts moving yet absent, faceless thoughts putting on a good face, facing each other's thoughts, is that what you really think? I don't know what I think...

...he said to be careful, people could get hurt, people somewhere peopling his thoughts, his thoughts of people, specific or general, a people of thought speaking their minds, hurting and thinking and being careful in their thought, careful in their hurting, I'm not *stupid* you know, I can think, thoughts lead so I can see what you're meaning, I can *see* what you're saying...

...and not knowing, can't know what's to come without thinking, she walks through the door, no, you walk through the door, a walk prepared to demonstrate your entrance, to show how you'll emerge into their thoughts, he/she sees you, the expectation of their thought of you preparing your walk, your entrance into life, you've walked into their lives, you're alive in their thoughts, you're prepared for their thoughts of you, walking slowly, deliberately, smiling, nonchalant...

...and the image opposite smiles back, a blurred half-formed thought of yourself drunk with talking, speaking about yourself, and how selfish you are in your thinking, your speaking of yourself, but after all you are significant, have much to say, people should listen, you listen to people so people should listen to you...

...but you don't think that you should, rather, you're embarrassed when you think of it, of how your speaking is so full of your thinking of yourself, pass the salt please, and he/she smiles but it's perfectly natural to talk about yourself, we all do it...

...and there are certain words you can't say over coffee and you wonder why, and when you try you find you can't think of those words, you can't think since those words are not part of the story of yourself you wish to think, thinking leads on, tells the story of yourself, or so you think, but over coffee those words resist thinking...

...she's coming through an open door again, no, it's you who are listening at the door hoping to hear their speaking, their speaking of their thoughts, perhaps they are thinking of *you*, but you can't hear...

...the telephone rings but you're not at home, you're seated somewhere else thinking about how often the telephone rings and why it's always late at night, don't people have anything better to do than phone you late at night, and what if you were sleeping or preparing for bed, in the shower or with a mouthful of food, can't people see how inconvenient is their thinking of you, how it puts you out of your mind?...

Ebisu

You watch them. They look normal, orderly, waiting for the doors to open, an air of anticipation and eagerness reflected from each face. Even when the doors open to allow entry, you notice they are polite, stepping aside at times to let the elderly or baby strollers pass in first.

"Good morning, shoppers. We're so glad you could join us at the Galleria."

That one doesn't require the fancier foods, you think, while watching her pick through limp asparagus, yellowed broccoli, you moving through the store at your own discretion, one hand on the shopping cart, the other encompassing the form lodged within your pocket.

"...bringing you the best at all costs..."

You must pass down various aisles in search of canned goods, bottled drinks, packaged powders— a storehouse of competitive consumer products. *What the hell is this?* reading: SOUL EXISTS... SCIENTISTS FIND HUMAN BODY WEIGHS .005 GRAMS LESS AFTER DEATH.

The slow-moving Syncop, isolated, unreachable, paces the iron catwalk high above the Galleria aisles, boots heard as a rhythm of watchfulness, has no needs, all nourishment collected from the air through a membrane covering its mouth. Occasionally its panoptic infra-red lenses indicate activity to be terminated, its left arm extends, a flash of light and the Galleria is spared, no costs of sales.

"Come on, we're going shopping," she could hear, but could not see the large hand grabbing hers, small and plasticine, the sensation of being dragged along in the dark, no tour guide, no mommy to describe to her the world of vision, the sudden shriek of the street closing down her ears momentarily. "Come on...", and rag-doll floppy legs scraping against concrete, "I just need some detergent," and the sense of others passing around her, tense, hungry, shopping, in her sightlessness feeling mother move away, leave her unguarded and suddenly hands occupy her space, snatch at desires above her head, at shelves above her head.

It was to be a new kind of supermarket, an out-of-town shopping arena where customers could compete for crisp vegetables, lean meat, fresh fish— offering tiered aisles with speed-ramps where an altercation could end in a fatal fall, the body of an inexperienced shopper coming to impress itself, face down into a bed of cabbage. The idea appealed to you. Your name is Spinne. You lost your soul when you placed it in a fish, *Ebisu*, to relieve your conscience, and your soul was taken from you, the fish now carried in another's hand, your soul gasping, the hand out of reach... *just a myth*, you try to rationalize, but someone's hand holds you, your soul carried along, images transmitted through fish eyes to you, images from where your soul's thief wanders: strollers on a beach, a slow luminous growth in air as mist rolls in from the sea, wordless dissolve of images amid your gasping thoughts, the strollers liquifying along the ocean's edge, and when your gaze finally focuses, you find... yourself standing in front of a display of asparagus, small unseen nozzles whispering a light spray of mist upon a half lit garden of green delight, inviting your hand to moisture, to reach for the bundled spears. Suddenly something pierces your palm, roots grow from your feet into the tiled aisles, chlorophyll eyes peer out upon tomatoes deflating like pricked balloons, punctures appearing on your hand form a luminous script— a vegetable neon implant of text spelling out the cost of casual desire: BREAK IT – YOU TAKE IT.

It's dark, always dark. Her little hand gropes along

the side of the shopping cart. *Mommy?* and someone rushing by her, her left elbow crushed into her ribs. Spinning and falling and "Mommy!", the sound of canned goods— a metallic thud upon the floor tiles— "Fuckin' cunt"— the sting across her cheek, cartilage cracking in her nose, the feeling of floor tile colliding with her skull, then the dark, the dark oozing down on to her lips.

"...our special today, shoppers, is fresh fillet of sole..."

Tight glass, the kind you bounce off, doesn't shatter, you think, while standing at the check-out counter gazing at the large vertical windows lining the walls of the shopping arena, when your gaze is interrupted by the face of a sneering cyborg in front of you. *No way out but through her,* having no credit chip, no money, your soul trapped somewhere in a fish, your hand quickly unleashing the stainless steel blade from your jacket pocket, splash of synthetic blood across the cashier's painted lips, *red on red!* you think retracting your hand with a snap, the cashier's eyes wide, unfocused, while you gasp for air grabbing your groceries from the conveyer belt— *I'm it!*— and remembering being a small boy playing hide and seek and hoping the other boys all liked you, at least more than Mom and Dad— *maybe behind that tree?*— and the mad dash to home-free home-free, the sense of never being close to one another, each boy moving from moment to moment, thing to thing, continually distracted, attention-span short, the imagined comradeship of friends disintegrating when you were left alone— *you're alone now*, you think and a moment later infra-red panoptics find you. Pushing yourself towards the automatic doors offering an exit, a ringing suddenly erupts in your ears, a ricochet of tight glass, bouncing crazily, slicing once, twice through the sleeve of your leather jacket—*Syncop*! and flashing through your mind the image of boots on a catwalk, visions of sushi throwing you into nausea...

...nausea (in a slow coming to consciousness), her right hand touching her left side, wet, the skin broken, something bony protruding from her chest-cage through the cotton fabric of her dress, slowly she props herself up with one arm, wanting to speak the word, one word to call out to her mommy, but she can't.

Can't see the Syncop... where is it?, as you negotiate the space behind the check-out counter, crouch close to the floor, inspect yourself— *no wounds, thank Ebisu*, and slip your hand beneath your jacket, extract the .38 from its holster, unclip the safety lock... *time to rock and roll*, and like a beetle scuttle close to the floor but move through the check-out counter alley back into one of the Galleria aisles, every now and then pausing briefly to gasp in large quantities of air...

how long before I drown?, attuning your ears to the air above, the subtle vibrations made by the slow foot-steps on an iron catwalk, not wanting to reveal any portion of your anatomy until your sense is acute, can hear the location of your target, home in on the plodding rhythm— *it's now or never* sings in your mind (from a phonograph record spinning in the room where as a small boy you sat listening perched upon the edge of your bed) trying to remember if it was Roy Orbison's voice, but thinking only of dark glasses, Syncop lenses, and in one continuous motion spin yourself onto your feet, without care for visual precision, swing your arms into scopic position, both hands confident of the cool steel between them, a tug at your pant cuff, and the deafening roar your ears have never become accustomed to... *What the...?* A figure falls from the catwalk and a soft mewling sound comes from the floor at your feet, the sensation of small hands gripping your pant-legs, the tip of your .38 smoking in fulfilment.

"Attention shoppers, security has been breached... please calmly vacate..."

The feeling is of coarse fabric covering a tensed leg, before a deafening noise shatters concentration, her grip suddenly released, the sensation of falling backwards, and before the anticipated slam against the floor tiles, two large hands slide under her armpits, jerk her from descent to ascent, the scent of musky skin as her little body is hugged to a large chest, her nose and mouth snuggled into a thick sweating neck. She has the immediate sensation of speed, the sound of running feet beneath her, vibrations from the body frame, the arms which secure her, and her ears pick out a faint "Let's go, little one," a dance of syllables before she once again falls into the senseless dark of enforced unconsciousness.

As you run, Spinne, you remember seeing mounds of mechanically separated chicken: breasts, legs, thighs; each unit perfectly adapted for frying; you remember sweet peppers, turnips, okra— and the sudden focus of your eyes stops you momentarily where a woman's torso is partially revealed, crushed beneath a fallen display of five-litre cans of lard, a hand twitching, grasping... and then comes the unlocked cacophony of screams issuing from the Galleria aisles as customers pursue their final purchase, bodies racing mindlessly refrigerated in a common dread of desire unmet, an alphabet soup of limbs gesturing, grabbing; and for a moment, you are dizzy, clasping to yourself a small body— *a minnow*, you think, as you leap over a turnstile labelled ENTER ONLY, reach the automatic doors, step over a bundle of groceries left in haste, reach the outside air, gasping in long breaths, holding your soulless self within your breast.

"Where to go from here?", she could hear muttered,

her little hands in a sudden panic of incomprehension grabbing at the leather jacket before them, her little mind trying to visualize... *mommy?*, trying to feel for her mommy, instead the feeling of leather, another holding her, thick arms encircling her...

So where's the beach, where do you like to swim little one?, you think, feeling the movement between your arms, sensing sun and sand in another's eyes, *ya, selva oscura*, just out of sight but not in your sights... yet.

The sound of rushing water against a shoreline, unfamiliar, not the comfortable environment of concrete and steel you're used to, Spinne, the streets you've passed through to get here, the speed streets full of counterfeit men and women coming and going in a continual stream, salmon fighting upstream, identical beings in an indefinite series, yet each one a mirror of all others, triumph of genetic replication... rushing water, and the vertigo of slowly drowning in air, you stop, are gazing across sand to where the thief stands, beside the water, fish in hand, poised, ready to cast your soul into the sea, *No!...*

Everything is ebbing, you feel it, the memory of mommy ebbing from your mind, the wetness ebbing from your numb chest-cage down your leg, and you're tired, so very tired, want to lie down, *please let me down*, your sightless eyes closing, everything ebbing away, dying in this moment, *please*?

Your eyes blurring in the intense sunlight, transferring the small body to your left arm, you crouch to one knee, your free hand automatically withdrawing the .38, then a sudden flashback through fish eyes of a stretch of beach, a crouched figure taking aim at you, holding a small limp bundle in one arm, your mouth gulping nothing but air.

While you watched from other eyes, you couldn't see the thief's other hand relieve itself of a sharp metallic object which spun, star shaped, towards your heart with the force of a man's weight, which buried itself between your ribs, between her ribs... you watched as the crouched figure with its small bundle dropped its well-aimed arm, collapsed upon the sand, you watched until you were both thrown into the sea where you both could begin to breathe again.

Phoning the Past

(Picking up the telephone book...)

Finally a few handshakes, pecks on the cheek, and then it's off to the aphonia of many voices talking in one head or one voice talking in many heads. Who to talk to this late at night?

Sometimes you are careful of what you wear, sometimes you don't care. They and you have changed.

"I lost all respect for you." Glass after glass of whiskey, erasing your yesterday, how you spoke, what was said, how badly you read, and it was *your* book launch. Nothing in common with them, except time, but you don't care, taking taxis home, body heat down, fantasies crawling over your skin. So what? The past, lost times. What if you connected? You connected. Self-congratulatory sound of paper pages turning, all the ideochatter and clinking of glasses:

there is only a trace of character having lived, personality having died.

(... I phoned the past.)

The coffee has gone cold. Time for a refill, time for a silence to invade the mouth. Can't talk. One touch, one kiss brings all perspective crashing down on to your writing table. "Hello?"

How the walls have changed colour, changed but remain redans against a catapulting of desire... "Hello?", I pick up the phone, sometimes you are careful... at least your tact is something you can hold on to... but your grip slips: "I lost all respect for you," and no words, your mouth a failure.

I wasn't supposed to continue that line, but late at night the orbiting drunkenness of desire spins with curiosity... "How are you?" and little insectoid noises at the other end of the line, the line you meant to continue, find out what has developed since then, little insectoid noises stockpiling the past.

When you picked up the phone, phoning the past, doomed by evanescence of another's voice, saying to you that it is dangerous to unmask images, when you picked up the phone you found yourself in a hyper-space without atmosphere, your voice floating apart from the necessity of speech, the necessity of words to resolve the story, set it right, make an ending happy.

But what a spectacle your voice made of itself, a spectacle for the ear of the beholder, and not beautiful but idiotic chatter, saying you're phoning from the past, each syllable crossing the line, the hyperspace without atmosphere, and yet the air of indifference, no hostility, just...

Finally a few handshakes, a few pecks on the cheek, and then alone in a taxi, not aware that the phone awaited you at home, that it was calling you and all the misplaced metaphors that constitute your life... they are deaf in their continual personating of themselves, their continuing fashioning of character: this one smokes a pipe. Is he learned? that one wears a wide brimmed fedora. Has Casanova come yet?

WATCH OUT! or you should have, but you had been organised according to the script for a disaster film, and your apprehension lost sight, while a complete culture including men, women and children, their gestures, languages and habits suddenly cryogenized in a glass coffin from the past...

"Hello?", darkness along the line, reaching your voice out towards an irreparable violence, towards all secrets, the towards itself coming back towards you, assuming its full meaning: the no longer of what it used to be, the crumbling voice of continuity.

You hadn't casually picked up the phone. You never casually pick up the phone. It lies in its cradle waiting for you and you know its demands, its need to be caressed, held tightly or held lightly according to your conversation. It listens closely or calls out loudly. Its scream reminds you of other atmospheres, atmospheres from the past in which you can no longer breathe, the air of the present in which you can hardly catch your breath, the fog of the future...

Many events never began, never existed, except in memory, and you could never document your memory for this reason, a reason apart from logic, could never document a linear life lived: 2 garages, 5 children, 3 TVs, well-to-do, upper middle-class with an ornamental housewife, an ornamental memory made according to cellular space.

The line you meant to continue went dead. They hung up, the past reproduced but beyond your grasp. Here cruelty is replaced with science: this is the way it was; and you cannot suffer resolution: you are cast in concrete, your image a statue, monumental but without thought, pressed down into a finely manicured lawn, your one hand cryogenized upon the receiver, mouth open, about to speak along the line, the "Hello?" of future generations phoning your past, studying your words, pasting together your continuity, admiring your image, reading your most recent unauthorized biography...

You lucky icon!

Fact Simile

Every day, a part of yourself becomes incomprehensible, a sudden straining away from the perpetual motion picture of biography, some part doesn't fit neatly, the uneasiness before the photograph, where no contemplation is possible. The photograph questions you, and directly.

What did you say? she thought while parked outside, refusing to go in. I can't go in, the absolute solitude of the parking lot, and where am I going anyway? she feeling always on the other side. "The event is you," he had said, but she couldn't believe it. I can't go in.

Outside was the vertigo of a flawless world, people walking effortlessly, the fantasy of a closed mental substance. She could almost touch it... digital perfection... just like at work, where her fingers encoded the hysteria of production, the production of information ground up into a synthetic deathless substance.

She was one of the many engaged in a continual procedure of directed information where the machine overrides all. She had to go in, level her gaze at the imaginary station, the glowing monitor like a face without recognition... Who are you? and key in the password, a four digit signifier of communication... SEND OUT PEOPLE TO GET SMASHED. What? A never innocent decision booting up the system, a type of absorption into the fantasy of a closed mental substance. I can almost touch it. Key in co-ordinates (the event is you), the other unnamed, never-mentioned thing, wishing for neutralisation and homogenisation of everybody else on Earth.

She felt it, the aura of an artificial menace, but then again that's exactly how the established order is, going to work every day, every day the same time, orchestrated rituals of hygiene, brushing your teeth, showering, the one egg and toast to break your fast. That's exactly how the established order proceeds, and on to work, orbital circulation, but you notice you've lost the feeling in your hands. I'm attached, she thinks, my hands are attached, really nothing biological since I can still feel my feet (and walking, I'm walking to work today, leave the car at home, no need to face the absolute solitude of the parking lot).

Like obsolescence in objects, you are appreciated, rewarded, a new full colour monitor, more sophisticated software, the verdict of fashion: every situation speaks of itself by denial. "No, I can't meet with you tonight, I'm too tired, and besides..." (you are obligated to make decisions while number-crunching, never innocent decisions, who to sleep with tonight? no contemplation is possible, everything condenses) "..."

Alone tonight, she listens for smash-ups from her balcony while sipping a gin and tonic (never innocent decision to drink); the panoptic decision of surveillance, a tactical hallucination she enjoys, the fingertips every day tapping out a universe of every threat to the senses, artificial prothesis through the nots and unnots where she can feel digital perfection, no longer the source of an absolute gaze.

She's blind and she knows it, but who needs eyes.

SEND OUT PEOPLE TO GET SMASHED. She can do that easily enough, simple order processing. What did you say? and then something not tactile, something like language heard, something that doesn't reproduce itself... and it's not like the uneasiness before a photograph, or the terror of credibility before the final montage from a perpetual motion picture of your biography...

Your biography breaks down: I can't go in. Outside now, outside of her self, something abstract moves away to where the distance is greater, and reflection is always possible.

Who's there? cautiously groping down the hallway from the kitchen to living room, the distance greater than you had decided (never innocent decision): the other unnamed, never-mentioned thing waits for you in your living room. Who's there? the question imagines and solicits you. She enters the room. No-one is there. Neutralized and homogenized, memory foreshadows everything. She sees the publicity holograms of her childhood shadowing themselves incessantly in their own image.

What did you say? approaching her television set. SEND OUT PEOPLE TO GET SMASHED, and she's travelling and small, she has small limbs, small feet, small hands, alone in the back seat of the car, her parents chatting, relaxed, driving to the grandparents' for Thanksgiving dinner, signs in languages cryptic flashing by on streets in ethnic neighbourhoods, an alien commerce which haunts all messages, (a tactical hallucination, she says to herself, that memory must be a tactical hallucination) the car suddenly imploding from the impact of another machine running a red light, glass in the face, small skull hitting the doorframe, everything condensing into pain, a universe of every threat to the senses.

She's blind and she knows it, the apparatus of surveillance at her unfeeling finger tips. She can't go in, until they come out, fetch her from the parking lot, wheel her chair into the building, position her before the monitor. She keys in: SEND OUT PEOPLE TO GET SMASHED! searching for the restoration of the real which escapes her, a memory which itself is the fiction of a universe saved, protected from pain: "the event is you," and the monitor blinks back: CATASTROPHIC ERROR.

Author's Notes

The Better Way. The title of this story is taken from the official slogan of the Toronto Transit Commission.

Skin Shoe, Long Pig. It was rumoured that during the late 19th and early 20th centuries in China, wealthy visitors from abroad could visit discreet eating establishments where they would be served the delicacy of 'long pig' or fresh, roasted human child.

Earfull. The events portrayed were experienced by the author during a weekend visit to friends in a small Southwestern Ontario town. After writing the work, the author received the following in the mail from his friends:

BACKYARD IS CRAWLING WITH WORMS

By The Canadian Press

It's a scene from a horror movie.

A resident of Selkirk, northeast of Winnipeg, says worms are so plentiful in his backyard that his lawn looks alive.

He asked not to be identified, to keep anglers away from the cornucopia of prospective bait.

He says he can hardly sleep at night because the worms make so much noise when they eat and rustle the leaves.

"It is like the whole yard is alive," he said. "The grass moves and the worms eat every leaf that has not been raked up from last year."

But he doesn't mind the worms.

"I added a little topsoil to the lawn so the ground would not be so hard for the worms to dig holes."

Ebisu is a sequel to *The Koi* by Oregon writer Misha. The mythical underpinning of both stories is the fish-cult belief that a man may place his soul in a fish, and in doing so his soul will remain pure while he can then go about any activity he wishes.

Richard Truhlar

Born on February 14, 1950, in Toronto, Richard Truhlar is a writer and text/sound/music composer. Along with other avant-garde Toronto writers, he was responsible for such imprints as Kontakte, Phenomenon Press, Tekstedítions and Underwhich Editions.

Throughout the 1980s, he championed the Underwhich Audiographic Series, publishing progressive audio sound recordings of sound poetry and electroacoustic music. Truhlar was a founding member of the sound poetry group OWEN SOUND and the electroacoustic chamber music ensemble TEKST. He is presently a member of the CEC (Canadian Electroacoustic Community) and the director of the contemporary music label Centrediscs at the Canadian Music Centre. *The Pitch* is his fifth major collection of literary works.